Julie's
B!g Mistake

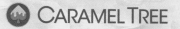

CARAMEL TREE

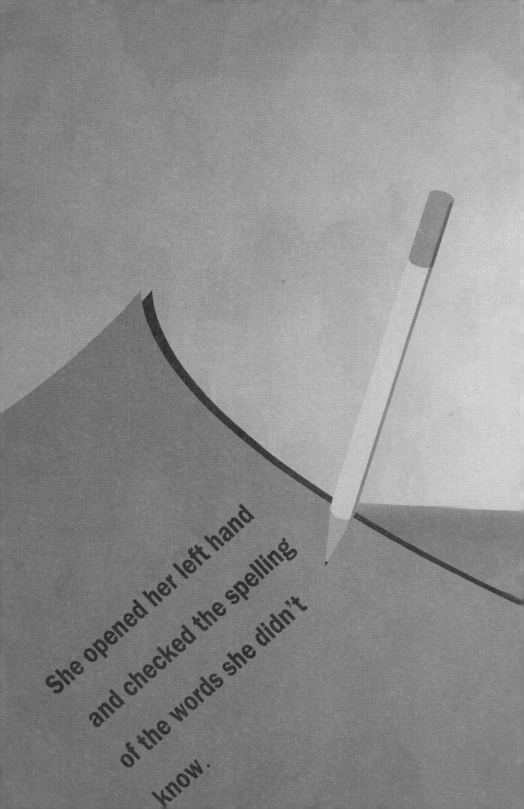

She opened her left hand and checked the spelling of the words she didn't know.

It was Monday morning and time to go to school. Julie sat at the back of the bus because she liked the up and down movements when the bus went over bumps. She also liked sliding from side to side when the bus turned around corners. At the next stop, Kelly got on and Julie's smiling face changed to a frown.

'Kelly McNeal,' Julie thought. *'Just looking at her can ruin a perfect morning.'*

Julie and Kelly had been competitors since kindergarten and now that they were in grade five, they were competing all the time. They were both good in math, sports, geography, and science, but when it came to spelling, the two of them were trying their hardest to be the best.

"Hi Julie," Kelly smiled. **"Are you ready for the BIG spelling test?"**

Julie smiled but didn't say anything. Inside she was getting very worried. *'The big spelling test?'* Julie thought. Julie had forgotten about the test, but she stayed calm. She looked at Kelly and said, "Sure. It will be an easy test," Julie lied.

Once they arrived at school, Julie ran into the girls' bathroom. She had a plan. She knew that it was wrong to cheat, but what could she do? She couldn't fail the test; she had to beat Kelly.

She locked herself into one of the stalls and took out her dictionary. With a black pen and a shaking right hand, she wrote four words on the palm of her left hand.

Julie walked to her classroom and sat down at her desk. The teacher, Mr. Rogers, walked in and handed out blank pages.

"Please write your name on the top right corner of the page," Mr. Rogers said. "This test is important."

Mr. Rogers said the first word. Julie knew it and wrote it down. She also knew the second word, but the third word she wasn't sure about. It was the same with the fourth and the fifth words. Julie didn't know how to spell them. She began to panic. She opened her left hand and checked the spelling of the words she didn't know.

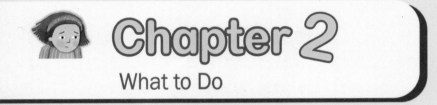

Chapter 2
What to Do

After school, Julie went home and sat on her favorite swing in the backyard. This was her place where she enjoyed being alone and thought about life. Today, she was troubled by what had happened. She didn't want to be alone, but what could she do? What would her parents think? She wanted to get up, jump off the swing, and run to her mom, but she couldn't. Julie knew she did something bad, and she was afraid to go and see her mom.

'They will never understand,' she thought. 'Why did I cheat?'

"Dinner is ready," Mom called. Julie felt as if she was caught eating cookies that she wasn't supposed to eat before meals. She felt guilty.

She didn't want to leave her swing; she didn't want to face her parents.

'Do they already know?' Julie thought and her hands trembled. 'How could they? Maybe someone had called and told them.'

Julie's thoughts were racing through her mind, and she finally dragged herself to the house, worried and concerned.

She slowly opened the living room door and looked inside. Nobody was there. She stopped and listened. After a few moments, she sneaked inside. Suddenly, the kitchen door opened and her mom yelled, "Dinner is... Oh, hi Julie. I didn't hear you come in. Will you help me set the table?"

'*She doesn't know,*' Julie thought. She was relieved and followed her mom into the kitchen.

When her brother, James, entered the kitchen, he looked at Julie and smiled.

'*Oh no! He knows,*' Julie thought suspiciously. '*He will tell on me.*'

Julie blushed and turned around. She couldn't face her brother. She trembled slightly, and her stomach felt like she was on a roller coaster.

Julie stared at the kitchen table and focused on her task. Setting the table helped her think of something different. She slowly set each plate, knife, and fork. Then she walked back to the cupboard and got four glasses.

She put three down on the table when suddenly her dad entered. Julie was so startled that she dropped the fourth glass. It fell on the table and rolled across the surface. It stopped for a short second at the edge and then fell down to the ground.

The glass exploded into many tiny pieces. Everybody stared at Julie.

"It's OK," Julie said. **"I'll clean up."**

"Be careful," Mom said and bent down to help Julie.

"So what happened at school today?" Dad asked when everyone sat down for dinner.

James answered first and talked about how exciting the math class was and how much he liked geography. He finished off with his favorite subject – sports. James especially loved running.

"I ran the one hundred meters in eleven point eight seconds. Yippy!" he yelled.

Julie listened with one ear. She was worried that her turn would come, and she wouldn't know what to say. She thought about the day and that awful moment when she had cheated on the spelling test.

'What if somebody saw me?' Julie thought.

"How about you, Julie?" asked Mom. "How was your day?"

All eyes turned to Julie, and she felt as if her family could see right through her. Julie felt they would find out her secret just by looking at her.

"N-n-nothing," she replied. "Nothing happened, just the usual," she lied.

Julie knew that nobody believed her. She was usually very talkative during dinner time. She liked her school very much and was always proud of what she did, except for tonight. She felt ashamed and didn't want to talk.

"What's wrong?" asked Mom. "Did something happen at school today?"

"No, nothing," she said. "I just don't feel so good." She lied again. She looked down at her plate and began to play with her food, but she still felt the eyes staring at her.

Chapter 4
Bad Dreams

Julie went to bed early, but she couldn't fall asleep. The wind was howling around her window, and it was almost as if she heard the wind say, *'You cheated. You will be caught.'*

She tossed back and forth for a while. Then she stood up and got a glass of water. As she drank some fresh cold water, she felt a little better.

Back in bed she slowly fell asleep, but then a nightmare came. She dreamed about standing in front of the principal in his large white office. Her mom was sitting on a chair, crying. Her dad was holding his head in his hands. The principal pointed at a large door, and Julie walked through it and found herself standing outside her school. She was alone, all alone.

Julie woke up with a scream and sat up in her bed, looking around.

"A dream," she said to herself. "It was just a dream."

In the morning, after she washed and got dressed, she went downstairs. She was very tired, and her eyes were red.

"What happened to you?" asked Mom when Julie stepped into the kitchen. "Your eyes are all red."

"Just bad dreams," Julie yawned.

"By the way, how was your spelling test yesterday?" asked Mom as she prepared sandwiches for the packed lunches.

'Oh no! She knows.' The thought shot through Julie's mind. *'She's testing me. Should I tell her? No!'*

Julie sat down slowly and said, "I don't know. We will find out the results today."

"Did you study enough?" asked Mom.

"Yes, I did," Julie lied again.

Julie quickly ate her breakfast and stood up. She got her backpack, put her lunch in it, and said goodbye to Mom and left for school.

"Have a good day," Mom hugged her and gave her a soft kiss. "Bye!"

When the English class started, Julie felt very sick. She sat quietly at her desk and waited for the teacher to enter. The door opened, and Mr. Rogers walked in. Julie sat up in her chair and stared at Mr. Rogers.

"Good morning," said Mr. Rogers. He sounded upset, and the classroom became quiet. "The spelling test results are terrible. Everybody failed except one."

He paused and looked around for a moment. "Julie,"

he finally said, and Julie felt as if a cold hand had

grabbed her from behind. She felt dizzy and when

she stood up, she moved back and forth.

"Congratulations," Mr. Rogers said with a smile. "You got all the words right."

Julie didn't say anything.

Julie looked around and saw Kelly, who looked angry and upset.

When Julie sat on the school bus going home, all she could think about was the test. She felt guilty. *'I cheated,'* Julie thought and looked out the window. She felt sad and lonely. She suddenly realized that her nightmare had become reality.

Lisa, one of her friends, sat beside Julie and said, "Well done, Julie. I will have to remember that trick. You weren't caught."

Julie stopped breathing, and her heart beat faster.

"What?" Julie asked, knowing exactly what Lisa meant.

"Nobody will find out from me," Lisa smiled and winked. "Did you see the look on Kelly's face?" Lisa teased.

Julie didn't remember how she stepped off the bus and how she entered the house. Suddenly, she was standing in the living room, looking around and feeling lost. She walked outside into the backyard and sat on her swing.

'Lisa saw me,' she thought. 'What if somebody else saw me, too? What should I do?'

She swung back and forth slowly. She knew that she had been wrong when she cheated. She had never cheated before and getting one hundred percent didn't mean anything now.

"I got one hundred percent because I cheated," Julie whispered. "I didn't get it because I was good. I am a cheater."

Tears filled her eyes, and she began to cry.

Julie was sitting in her room and thinking about all the bad things that had happened since she cheated. She had lied four times to her parents, and she had felt sick and miserable. Julie felt like a cheater, and she had terrible nightmares. Her mind was made up, and she searched for her mom. *'I need help,'* Julie thought.

Julie went downstairs where she heard her mom cooking in the kitchen. She stood by the kitchen door for a while and watched her mom prepare dinner.

'What will she think?' Julie thought. 'Will she still love me?'

Finally, Julie found her courage and said, "Mom, can we talk?"

"Any time, Julie," replied Mom. "I always feel it when there is something wrong."

Mom looked at Julie and saw the tears in her eyes. They walked into Julie's bedroom and sat on her bed.

"What is it?" Mom asked.

Julie took a deep breath and replied, "I cheated on the spelling test."

Mom looked at her silently for a moment and shook her head slowly. She was disappointed with Julie. Mom asked, "And? What do you want to do now? You know that it was wrong."

"Yes, I do. It was wrong, I know, but I didn't study and I didn't know what to do. I didn't want to fail the test. Then I lied to you. Now I got one hundred percent, but I still feel miserable." Julie began to cry.

"It's good that you know your mistake, but what do you plan to do now?" Mom asked again.

"I don't know. I'm scared." Julie looked at her mom. Tears were running down her cheeks.

"Well, you cheated, Julie. What do you think you should do?" asked Mom.

"Do I have to talk to Mr. Rogers and confess?" Julie asked.

"I think that would be right," said Mom.

"But what if I am thrown out of school?" Julie was very worried. "What about Dad?"

"You'd better talk to him yourself," said Mom.

Dad was very upset with Julie after she told him everything. She wasn't allowed to watch any television for a month. He was very angry, and he was walking up and down the living room as Julie left for her bedroom.

Julie cried silently in her room, but she was relieved that she had told her parents. The feeling of lying to them bothered her the most. She would have to go and tell Mr. Rogers tomorrow. Then all her classmates would find out.

Julie tried not to think of how Kelly would react. The next day would be another difficult day, but she knew that she had to do it. She had to fix her big mistake. Julie promised herself that she would never make the same mistake again. She knew she would never cheat.

Julie got ready for bed and fell asleep quickly.

She didn't have any more nightmares.